Purchased with Book Fair Funds   1995

D0124289

W9-BTC-210

CLARA JOINS THE CIRCUS

To librarians, parents, and teachers:

Clara Joins the Circus is a Parents Magazine READ ALOUD Original — one title in a series of colorfully illustrated and fun-to-read stories that young readers will be sure to come back to time and time again.

Now, in this special school and library edition of *Clara Joins the Circus*, adults have an even greater opportunity to increase children's responsiveness to reading and learning — and to have fun every step of the way.

When you finish this story, check the special section at the back of the book. There you will find games, projects, things to talk about, and other educational activities designed to make reading enjoyable by giving children and adults a chance to play together, work together, and talk over the story they have just read.

For a free color catalog describing Gareth Stevens' list of high-quality books, call 1-800-542-2595 (USA) or 1-800-461-9120 (Canada). Gareth Stevens' Fax: (414) 225-0377.

Parents Magazine READ ALOUD Originals:

A Garden for Miss Mouse
Aren't You Forgetting
    Something, Fiona?
Bicycle Bear
Bicycle Bear Rides Again
The Biggest Shadow in the Zoo
Bread and Honey
Buggly Bear's Hiccup Cure
But No Elephants
Cats! Cats! Cats!
The Cat's Pajamas
Clara Joins the Circus
The Clown-Arounds
The Clown-Arounds Go
    on Vacation
The Clown-Arounds Have
    a Party
Elephant Goes to School
The Fox with Cold Feet
Get Well, Clown-Arounds!
The Ghost in Dobbs Diner
The Giggle Book
The Goat Parade

Golly Gump Swallowed a Fly
Henry Babysits
Henry Goes West
Henry's Awful Mistake
Henry's Important Date
The Housekeeper's Dog
I'd Like to Be
The Little Witch Sisters
The Man Who Cooked
    for Himself
Milk and Cookies
Miss Mopp's Lucky Day
No Carrots for Harry!
Oh, So Silly!
The Old Man and the
    Afternoon Cat
One Little Monkey
The Peace-and-Quiet Diner
The Perfect Ride
Pets I Wouldn't Pick
Pickle Things
Pigs in the House
Rabbit's New Rug

Rupert, Polly, and Daisy
Sand Cake
Septimus Bean and His
    Amazing Machine
Sheldon's Lunch
Sherlock Chick and the
    Giant Egg Mystery
Sherlock Chick's First Case
The Silly Tail Book
Snow Lion
Socks for Supper
Sweet Dreams, Clown-Arounds!
Ten Furry Monsters
There's No Place Like Home
This Farm is a Mess
Those Terrible Toy-Breakers
Up Goes Mr. Downs
The Very Bumpy Bus Ride
Where's Rufus?
Who Put the Pepper in the Pot?
Witches Four

Library of Congress Cataloging-in-Publication Data

Pellowski, Michael.
    Clara joins the circus / by Michael Pellowski ; pictures by True
Kelley.
        p. cm. -- (Parents magazine read aloud original)
    Summary: Clara Cow, in search of excitement, tries to join the
circus but seems hopelessly unsuitable for almost every job.
    ISBN 0-8368-0998-X
    [1. Circus--Fiction. 2. Cows--Fiction.] I. Kelley, True, ill.
II. Title. III. Series.
PZ7.P3656Cl 1995
[E]--dc20   94-34653

This North American library edition published in 1995 by Gareth Stevens Publishing, 1555 North RiverCenter Drive, Suite 201, Milwaukee, Wisconsin, 53212, USA, under an arrangement with Pages, Inc.

Text © 1981 by Michael Pellowski. Illustrations © 1981 by True Kelley. Portions of end matter adapted from material first published in the newsletter *From Parents to Parents* by the Parents Magazine Read Aloud Book Club, © 1989 by Gruner + Jahr USA Publishing, New York; other portions © 1995 by Gareth Stevens, Inc.

Printed in the United States of America

1 2 3 4 5 6 7 8 9 99 98 97 96 95

To my wife, Judy, and my sons, Morgan and Matthew – M. P. To Auntie Barb True – T.K.

CLARA
JOINS THE
CIRCUS

by Michael Pellowski
pictures by True Kelley

Parents Magazine Press / New York

Gareth Stevens Publishing / Milwaukee

Clara Cow was bored.
Every day she got up at dawn.
She nibbled grass all day.
She went to bed at sunset.
Nothing exciting ever happened.

One afternoon, Clara heard strange noises.
She went up the hill to have a look.

From the hilltop, Clara saw a circus parade.
The Ringmaster, who was leading the parade,
shouted, "Halt!"
The parade stopped.
"We'll camp here," said the Ringmaster.

"Circus life must be exciting,"
said Clara to herself.
"I wonder if I could join."
So she walked down the hill into the circus camp.
She came face to face with the Ringmaster.

Clara smiled. "My name is Clara.
I'd like to join the circus."
The Ringmaster said,
"We're always looking for new acts.
What can you do?"

Clara gulped. "I've never worked
in a circus," she said.
"I don't know WHAT I can do."

"Don't give up," the Ringmaster told her.
"You'll have a chance to try out."

"I'll try my best," Clara promised.
"I want to join the circus
more than anything."

"Good," said the Ringmaster.
"Let's start with tightrope walking."

Clara climbed the ladder.
She stepped out on
the thin, tight line.
"Oh-oh," Clara said.
She began to wobble.
The rope began to wobble.
"Whoops!" cried Clara. "Help!"

Ker-splash!
Clara tumbled off the tightrope
right into a tub of water.
"Well, so much for tightrope walking,"
Clara said. "What's next?"

"Juggling," said the Ringmaster.
Clara picked up three heavy wooden pins.
She tossed them into the air
and tried to juggle.

Bonk! Bonk! Bonk!
One by one the pins landed
on Clara's head.
"Ouch! Ouch! Ouch!" she moaned.
"I guess I can't juggle either.
Maybe I'm a trapeze artist."

Soon Clara was high
above the center ring,
hanging from a trapeze.
"Here I go!" she yelled.

But Clara wasn't a trapeze artist.
Nibbling grass all day had
made her too heavy.
The ropes snapped.
Down came the trapeze.
Down came Clara Cow—
into the safety net.

"Now what?" asked the Ringmaster.
Clara thought a minute.
"I'll be the first cow to be shot
out of a cannon," she said.
The Ringmaster shook his head
as Clara climbed into the cannon.

Halfway in, Clara got stuck.
"Get me out of here!" she hollered.
A great big elephant came to Clara's rescue.
She wrapped her trunk around Clara
and pulled and pulled and pulled.

Finally, out popped Clara.
"Why don't you help me set up tents?"
the elephant suggested.
"I'll try," said Clara.
So off they went.

But when Clara aimed to hit a peg,
she hit her foot instead.
"YEOW!" she bellowed.
"No," said the Ringmaster.
"She can't set up tents either."

"Please," begged Clara.
"Give me another chance."
"There aren't many jobs left,"
said the Ringmaster.
"Do you want to be a lion tamer?"
"No, thank you!"
Clara quickly answered.

"How about being the target for the knife thrower?"

"I don't think so," Clara replied.

"I can't think of anything else,"
said the Ringmaster.
"She could sell peanuts and popcorn
to the crowd," the elephant suggested.
"I know I could do that!" cried Clara.
"Well, all right," agreed the Ringmaster.

Clara went into the main tent.
The Ringmaster gave her a uniform
to wear and a tray filled with bags
of peanuts and popcorn.
"Walk across the tent and
into the stands," he told her.
"Let me hear you yell,
'Peanuts and popcorn!'"

Eagerly Clara walked toward the stands.
She did not look where she was going.
Just as she passed the doorway,
the clowns came rushing in.
Clara didn't see the clowns.
"Oh, no!" cried the Ringmaster.

HA!

Bump! Smash! Crash!
Clara went flying this way.
Clowns went flying that way.
Peanuts and popcorn went flying
every which way.
Luckily no one was hurt.

Suddenly, the Ringmaster began to laugh.
Soon everyone in the tent was laughing.
"What a great entrance,"
said the Ringmaster.

39

"We'll make that accident the opening
of the clown act," said the Ringmaster.
"It will be terrific. Will you do it?"

"You mean I can join the circus?" said Clara.

"You sure can," said the Ringmaster.

"Ya-hoo!" shouted Clara.

And that is how Clara Cow
joined the circus.

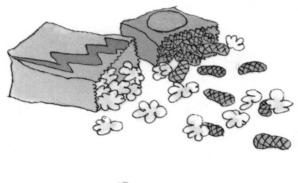

Notes to Grown-ups

Major Themes

Here is a quick guide to the significant themes and concepts at work in *Clara Joins the Circus*:

- Ambition: Clara found something that she really wanted to do.
- Willingness to try: who knows what someone can accomplish until he or she tries?
- Fun: at the end of the story, the fun of the circus is doubled for Clara when she turns her accidental fall into the talent that gets her a job with the circus.

Step-by-step Ideas for Reading and Talking

Here are some ideas for further give-and-take between grown-ups and children. The following topics encourage creative discussion of *Clara Joins the Circus* and invite the kind of open-ended response that is consistent with many contemporary approaches to reading, including Whole Language:

- This story demonstrates that what you *can* do is more important than what you can't. Clara's failures at the athletic acts didn't matter at all in the end; they helped her eliminate what she couldn't do, thereby discovering what she could do.

- Might Clara have learned any of the circus acts if she'd practiced them? Her size and weight were too much for the high wire and the trapeze, but could she have learned to juggle?

- Clara was afraid of being a lion tamer and of being the knife thrower's target. Why was she more afraid of those jobs than of the trapeze? Another person might be afraid of heights, but not of lions. We all have fears, but each of us is afraid of different things. This might be an opportunity to talk over any fears your child may have.

Games for Learning

Games and activities can stimulate young readers and listeners alike to find out more about words, numbers, and ideas. Here are more ideas for turning learning into fun:

Alliteration Game

Alliteration (e.g., <u>C</u>lara <u>C</u>ow) is commonly used in children's books to heighten appeal and make a character's name easy to remember. Children enjoy the repetition of initial consonant sounds. You can review the alphabet together with an alliteration game. As you go through the alphabet, take turns thinking of alliterative animal names (e.g., <u>A</u>lbert <u>A</u>lligator, <u>B</u>ernard <u>B</u>ear). Continue the game until one person cannot think of an example. To make the game more interesting, start your review of the alphabet at different letters.

Circus Popcorn

You and your child can make a yummy batch of Circus Popcorn together, using popcorn and peanuts like those sold by Clara Cow in this story.

Pop approximately 3 quarts (3 liters) of popcorn. Put the popped corn and some peanuts into a large paper bag that has been sprayed with a nonstick cooking spray. Combine the following ingredients in a pan and bring to a boil, stirring once or twice:

- 1/2 cup (.12 l) butter or margarine
- 1/4 cup (.06 l) light corn syrup
- 1/2 teaspoon (2.5 milliliters) salt
- 1 cup (.24 l) brown sugar

Continue boiling the mixture for three minutes, and then add 1/2 teaspoon (2.5 ml) baking soda. Pour the foamy mix over the popcorn and peanuts in the bag. Microwave the mix for three minutes, shaking the bag after each minute to coat the popcorn and peanuts. Carefully spread the Circus Popcorn onto a cookie sheet lined with foil and let the mixture cool. Then break the popcorn mix apart, eat, and enjoy!